I STILL HEAR THE DRUMS

Linda Lewis Everett

Author

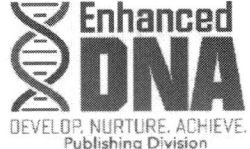

I Still Hear the Drums

Copyright © 2019 Linda Lewis-Everett

All rights reserved.

No portion of this publication may be reproduced, stored in any electronic system, or transmitted in any form or by any means without the written permission from the author. Brief quotations may be used in literary reviews.

Cover Design by Marvin Rhodes, Jr
MR Design

ISBN-13: 9781733647731

DEDICATION

I dedicate this book to the memory of my dear sister Debra. I love you with every inhale and exhale I take. Because of you sister, I have no fear.

Dedicated to the memory of my mother, Daisy Williams Lewis. Like we always said mama, "me and you always together."

Dedicated to my father, Chester Lewis Sr. Your love for me was immeasurable, I get it now, daddy.

Dedicated to my husband Dubois Everett - the man that I love, and the man that loves me.

Dedicated to my only son, Kenneth A. Peters. I held you on my chest for a few months, but will hold you in my heart for eternity.

Dedicated to my Grandlady, Jala Peters. I love you dearly, I always will.

Dedicated to all of my brothers and sisters - because of you, I am. "Ubuntu".

Dedicated to all of my precious nieces and nephews whom I love as my own.
Dedicated to all the souls lost at sea during the Middle Passage

SPECIAL DEDICATION
KENNETH ANTHONY PETERS

A heartfelt thank you to the front cover model; my Son Kenneth Anthony Peters.

The depiction of a Black Man beating the drum, births the possibility of us ALL hearing the tribal DRUMS. My hope is that everyone will have the opportunity to visit the African continent and hear the DRUMS.

I will love you ALWAYS Son.

Linda Lewis-Everett

FOREWORD

by

Gloria Lewis-Vaughn

Perhaps you have felt as though something was missing, a vital piece, a critical missing link...a bit of the story yet unspoken, the song that cries "Undone."

...The piece to the puzzle that would fill the void. A memory just out of reach, outside your grasp, yet within view, off, far off in the distance.

The piece, the part, the memories which brings it all full circle, and skillfully, yet painfully connects the dots, the tears and the fears.

A universal piece; pain on paper with bits of joy interspersed. A Sound.

Here... now... it is in your hands, I STILL HEAR THE DRUMS

History, Our History, Uniquely Ours, Pridefully and Painfully Ours, Steadfast and Immovably Ours. Needful and Timely it is Ours.

Linda Lewis-Everett, in her debut novel, has birthed a work

replete with a range of emotions which usher the reader into a rich relationship with the characters, who leap off the page and into the heart.

You will instantly and effortlessly become immersed in the familiar journey revisited, where hope is non-negotiable.

Shh, whenever I quiet myself... I STILL HEAR THE DRUMS.

Gloria Lewis-Vaughn

Author, Lessons Learned On My Way Home-2003

THOUGHTS THAT MADE ME WRITE THE NOVEL:

As we search the essence of who we are it is imperative to know from whence we came.

It is often said that to know where you are going you have to know from where you have come.

I pose the question: How do we know, if no one has ever told us, or if what we were told, were untruths?

Sometimes soul-searching is deliberately sabotaged by us not wanting to uncover our finds.

This novel is an attempt to reach back, walk along side, and point a clear direction.

I pray you enjoy this journey, of a people!

Linda Lewis-Everett

Linda Lewis-Everett

TABLE OF CONTENTS

Chapter 1	CAPTURED	Page # 1
Chapter 2	BROKEN IN	Page # 12
Chapter 3	FREEDOM, NOW WHAT?	Page # 29
Chapter 4	THE NEWS IS TRUE	Page # 35
Chapter 5	THE CIVIL WAR	Page # 40
Chapter 6	THE BIG NEWS	Page # 44
	EMANCIPATION PROCLAMATION	
Chapter 7	GOODBYE TO AFRICA	Page # 53
Chapter 8	A BRAND NEW HOME	Page # 56
Chapter 9	LAST DAYS	Page # 61
Chapter 10	THE DRUMS USHERING ME HOME	Page # 64
	EPILOGUE	Page # 65
	AFRICA IN PICTURES	Page # 66

CHAPTER 1

CAPTURED

I hear my tribal sounds from the distant shores. I faintly hear them now if I press my ear squarely on the splintered boards.

They're hard to make out over the thrashing waters but I know what they are saying "You are not lost to us. Wherever you end up you still belong to us!"
"Us" is Ghana, Senegal, Sierra Leone, and Cameroon. You are, and will always be Africa! Yes child, you are Africa.

The sounds are becoming really faint now. I don't think I hear our drums. I lie very still and hold my breath, hoping to hear my drums. My drums from home. I no longer hear them. I no longer hear the drums.
I'm sure now, I no longer hear the drums. Oh God, I no longer hear those drums! I lie there listening to all sorts of sounds but none that comfort me. I hear only constant moans and groans. That's all I hear now, no more drums.

The smell of my homeland flower is also gone from me. The beautiful vibrant and fragrant flowers that were tossed in the sea behind me, the scent that wafts thru my village.

The scent of home is gone now too. I smell only fear now. Fear and death have now taken over my senses.

I don't hear my drums or smell any familiar scents, but I'm not yet afraid. I'm not yet afraid, for many nights in my homeland I was told of these long journeys. The journeys across the waters with my people never to return. I was told of other family and people from my village that crossed through the door of no return. My elders assured me and all the youth in my village that they wouldn't rest until all were returned.

My elders are mighty Kings and Chiefs, and Queens, so I'm not yet afraid. My elders have rescued me from many a snare before. My elders will surely rescue me soon. I know this for sure. I'm not yet afraid!

Moaning and groaning, weeping and wailing from all sides. Yet, I lie quiet and still. I hear voices calling out, day and night but I don't understand what they are saying. I wish to answer back, to tell them my elders will be here soon, I want to tell them not to worry. But I am yet quiet, I am yet still. I don't think they will understand me when I speak. I don't recognize any sounds I hear. They may not understand me either. So I will just lie here and wait. Wait for my elders.

I close my eyes in hopes it closes my mind. I can't bear to think of me not returning home. I can't let my mind torture me with such thoughts; thoughts of never seeing my family. Never singing and dancing to the setting sun, never watching my elders teach me and all the other youth our ways and customs. No I can't let those thoughts in.

My elders say your mind can be your worst enemy only if you let it. Today I will not let it.
I will hold fast to the promise that rings in my heart, that they will never forget me. I know in my heart I will never forget them.

I close my eyes and think of nothing but home. Nothing but Africa!

I'm awakened by more crying, more stench, and more death. The smells make me sick and I vomit all on myself and the person lying next to me. They don't even move! I am too weak to move so I just lie there in the vomit, embarrassed and sad.

I haven't recognized a sound since leaving my village, other than the sounds of crying. I guess cries are the same wherever you find yourself. The crying goes on all day and all night. I haven't cried yet!

There's someone chained to me, I believe she is of the nearby village. She looks like them, with her dark brown skin, large eyes and very high cheekbones. She's quite pretty. I can see her face when the light shines through. She has been crying and thrashing about the entire time. I try to comfort her with my eyes. We are chained so I can't hold her, or rock her, to let her know we will be fine.
She tries to speak to me thru her bouts of sobbing but I don't understand what she is saying. I may not understand her words but I do know what her eyes are saying... I want to tell her not to be afraid, when my elders come for me, we will all be returned home.

Home to our villages safely.

I am yet quiet though. I lie there and wonder how long before the elders find me. How much more of this torture can we all take?

DAYLIGHT STILL DARK THOUGH

Daylight finds its way to my face thru the holes and cracks of the ship. There are a few less people down here now. I believe the older ones died and were tossed overboard. I cried myself to sleep.

This is the 7th or 8th day since leaving Africa, I'm not sure anymore. I try to remember how many sunrises and sunsets I've seen to keep up with the days. I keep thinking of my people and I keep telling myself I'm not yet afraid! 7 or 8 sunrises is not too long for my elders, they will find me, I'm sure of it. Sleep finally comes!

I awaken to the fact that I am still bound. Bound to people who look like me, but I don't know and they don't know me. What I do know is they are frightened and confused. I see it in their eyes when the sun finds its way to us. The fear is the first thing I see. The sun is brief and fleeting but it allows me to see them. I believe it has now been over 40 sunrises since leaving my home. I can barely move my head to catch the sun as it sneaks thru the cracks. I am weaker than I've ever been in my life! The food they force us to eat smells worse than the stench of the ship so I don't eat much. On the days I refuse to eat, the white men force the vile food down my throat. I throw the slop right back up. I smell of vomit, urine and bowel; I smell very bad. I smell like everybody else on this ship. The putrid smell is everywhere, and on all of us.

Being cramped on this ship so long my body seems as if it is betraying me now. I am now only flesh and bones, all my weight has gone from me. I don't even recognize this body any longer. My body is limp, bruised, battered, and frail. The only thing that remains is the color. The rich color of my African people has not left my skin. The "me" I once knew is now gone.

At night I think if this is a bad dream, it's gone on too long but I know it isn't a dream, or a nightmare. I know this is real. I am in the bottom of a ship, packed with hundreds of people who look like me, headed to a place we've never been before. A place that I have always heard of and feared! Quietly I say to myself, "God this can't be happening to me", but it is.

I must remember my people are very smart, crafty, powerful, and brave, so I yet believe they will find this ship and find me. They will return me back to my family and help the others on this ship find their way home too!
I hope the others on this ship have elders looking for them, as well. The white men have large weapons, but my elders have many powerful weapons too. We are skilled with many weapons and are quite brave. I am calmed by my thoughts of being rescued, I will close my eyes again but sleep will not come. The constant crying, moaning and wailing keeps sleep from me. The deep pain in my bones also keeps me awake day and night. It's hard to tell day from night at the bottom of this ship.

I try to sleep but the same nightmare keeps waking me up. Run, Abena run! I'm running as fast as my young legs can carry me. Running through the high grass, not stopping to look where I'm going. Just running from the white intruders. I'm one of the fastest runners in my village. Faster than all the girls, and most of the boys. I'm not running a race today, I'm running to save my life!

The next thing I know there are 4 or maybe five white intruders standing over me. I'm fighting as best I can but they are too strong. One of the men grabs me by my hair and hits me in the head with a large club! When I wake up I have chains on my hands and feet. I wake up bloody, with one of the men on top of me doing things he shouldn't be doing. I try to cry out but he covers my mouth to silence my cries. When he is finished the others get on top of me and do their business too. All the while they are laughing and grinning. Their sweat and stench makes me vomit. When the last white man is done raping me, I'm soaked with blood and sweat. The blood is running warm down my legs, and the salty sweat from the men is in my eyes and mouth. I try to rise up, and I'm hit in the head again. When I awake, I'm still on the ship. It wasn't a nightmare. This is really happening!

I've seen sunrise 48, 49, maybe even 50 times. I don't really know anymore. Many more people have died and been thrown overboard. I believe I will pretend to be dead so I can be thrown overboard. Once overboard I may be able to swim back home! I was once a great swimmer. I was once both fast and strong. That time seems like years ago, but I believe it was only 40 something days ago. My body is weak now, and I probably couldn't make it all the way back home.

THE TAKE OVER

I hear a lot of loud noises and quick steady movement above me. Maybe my elders have found me. Oh, God I hope it is my elders! They will be so proud to see I stayed strong. I believed in them. I believed they would find me. Oh, God I can't wait to see their faces. Faces like mine; dark from the many hours of sun, faces that are beautiful and strong. Faces that I've missed! Oh, God only knows how much I've missed them.

My heart is bursting inside, bursting with joy; sheer joy that I will be home soon.

I knew this day would surely come. Now that my elders are here we can help all the others find their way back to their villages. I am so proud of my elders. I know they will grab me up and place kisses on my face. Abena Imari will be home soon, I just know I will.

Oh joy, oh sweet joy I feel knowing I will soon be back home again. I don't think I could spend another day on this ship.

Now, to know that my family is finally here to take me home. I can smell all the scents of home now. The high grass that I ran through every morning that smells like lemons, it even tastes like lemons as I sometimes put the blades of grass in my mouth while sitting alone in the grass daydreaming. Oh, and I can smell the flowers that cover the mountain side. The smell from every home leaves me wanting to run in and eat at each table! I think I will do just that when I get home! I will stop by all the homes in my village and sup with everyone. They will be so glad to see me.

I haven't eaten much since being taken. I will probably eat all of my family's portions.

Well the sounds seem to be getting louder overhead. I believe it won't be long now! Not long now, my heart is beating so fast it may just beat straight out of my chest!

I hear the scuffling of people and the sound of chains clanging and banging about. The loud talking that I don't understand seems to be getting louder.

I'm confused now! The white men that captured me are standing right here in front of us! Where are the elders! What did they do with my elders? I don't believe they were overpowered. My elders are stronger and smarter than these men! My elders are warriors. My dad and brothers are warriors!

I know in my soul they didn't overtake my people! I know that in my soul!

I now know that my elders were never here!

A NEW LAND

Many days of the same thing, beatings, rapes, killings, throwing people overboard. Nothing changes. We are still in the bottom of a slave ship at sea.

I see land now. How glad I am to see land. I think it's been 53 or 54 sunrises but, now finally land. To put my feet on solid ground, to stand, to walk, to stretch, to run! Oh, how I thank you God we have finally reached land. Oh, but what kind of land is this? It is very unfamiliar.

Yelling and pushing, whipping and beating. The white men that captured us are pushing and shoving us off the ship. I only see white people. I don't see any of my people, no Africans other than the ones in chains, and shackles. I don't see any of my elders. Where are they? Where are my elders! They said they would always protect us.
My heart is heavy and I am beginning to feel sick. The slop the white man forced me to eat earlier today is now working its way up and is now spewing from my mouth onto the person in front of me! The force of it lands on me, and I don't flinch. I've grown used to it and used to the smell now. The smell of my own vomit, and the smell of all those around me.

I now feel lightheaded as if I am going to faint. I've never felt this sick before. I am now very sick, sick and very afraid!

THE AUCTION BLOCK

We are pushed and prodded and herded to a desolate place, then stripped completely of the sparse garments we have on. The men and boys are on one side and the women and young girls are shoved to another side.

I can now see just how many people were on the ship. Not an exact count because so many died and were tossed overboard on the way here. Not sure where "here" even is. I've never seen a place like this before.

I look around and see some of the women are with child. Some of them are as frail as I am, and some look even worse! They look as if they may hit the ground at anytime.
I see girls that may be my same age. Girls I would certainly have played with if we were all back home. But we're not.
One of the white men drags me to a small box and begins looking at every part of my body. I'm embarrassed as he spreads my legs apart, opens my mouth, and looks at my young frail body. A tear runs down my face and runs into my mouth, the taste of my tears are salty.

I'm more ashamed of my tears than I am of being naked. Then more white men come over to me, looking at me and touching all over me. They are talking to each other but I don't understand a word they are saying.

One man smiles and grabs me off the small box and throws me in the back of a wagon. There are more people already in the wagon. I look around at each face to see if I see anyone that looks familiar, anyone from home. I don't know any of them. Another level of sadness sweeps over me.

Most of the people in the wagon are men. They all look like they were once strong and maybe even warriors. I guess the ship, and the long journey from their home has beaten the warrior out of them. None of them looks me in my eyes as I climb into the back of the wagon. No one attempts to comfort me as I begin to cry. I pray for death to come now. I pray that I see not the elders, but the ancestors that are long gone. I don't believe I can stand much more. Death would be a welcome sight for me right now. I don't believe I will see my home ever again. I won't see home with the beautiful mountains, I won't see the baby gazelle as she races thru the field. I won't see the animals that are as much at home there as we are. I already miss the flowers, the grass the trees, the life, my life! I miss home, I miss my mother, I miss my father, my brothers and sisters. I miss the sound of the drums!

CHAPTER 2

BROKEN IN

I've been bought and sold twice and left behind four babies each time. Had a total of eight babies. Seven living and one dead. The first time I was sold off without my babies liked to killed me. I never dreamed I'd still be alive today. Not after all the beatings I've had. They almost killed me because I wasn't gonna leave my babies.

Lord, the first time old Master come to me and tell me to bring him my baby boy I didn't know exactly what he wanted with him. That was my firstborn baby. I was only about fifteen years old when he was born. I really can't remember who the daddy was because Master would send men in every night to lay with me. I remember the first time Master sent a buck in to lay with me I was pretty scared. I had never been with a man before in that way. My only knowing about a man was from being raped in the bottom of that slave ship. Back home you would have to be joined together and blessed by your elders before you could come together sexually. Things surely ain't nothing like back home. Master just send anybody he wants to your shack and you have to do your business with them, or else. The first time I realized I was carrying a baby I really missed my mama. My mother would have told me all the things to do for my baby. Being that I'm all the way over here by myself, I just learn as I go. One thing for sure I tell you, this here baby is all the family I got here in America so I'm going to love on this baby like no child ever been loved. That I know for sure.

This little brown eyed brown boy looks up at me with so much love, that it breaks my heart to know he's gonna grow up in such a horrible place. It breaks my heart to know there ain't nothing I can do about it. Lord, help me to look after my baby please. I say that every day and every night.

Some nights I whisper in his ear and tell him the stories of home. The stories of Africa. I tap my leg to make the sound of the drums so he will know about the drum beat. So he will know about home.

I named my little boy Kwame, same as my father. He looks just like my father! I'm sure my mother and father would love little Kwame. When the Master comes he changes his name to Roy, but I still call him Kwame.

Master changes my name too. He calls me Beulah, and that's the name I go by now. Not Abena Imari, not the name that was given to me by family. I go by the name my Master gave me when I arrived on his plantation. I still know who I am and where I belong. I am Abena Imari, from the Continent of Africa. There's nothing he can do to change that!

Today is like every other day when Master calls for me to come up to the big house, but this time he tells me to bring

Kwame, or Roy when I come. Don't know why Master want to see my little Kwame but I do as I'm told and bring Kwame up to the big house. A few white men are standing around and one of them snatches Kwame right out of my arms! I grabs my baby right back from him and the next thing you know Master pulls the whip out and slashes it across my back. The force and pain of the whip drops me straight to the ground. I bounce back up as quickly as I fall and race after the white man with my little boy. The whole time I'm running, Master is behind me beating me with the whip. The pain of losing my baby is much worse than this whip so I keep right on running trying to get my Kwame back. Master steps on my back when I fall this time. I lay there watching the wagon ride off with my baby, with my only family. How in the world is Kwame gonna make it without me. How in the world am I gonna make it without Kwame. No more fight left in me, but Master continues to beat me anyway. He's beating me for loving my flesh and blood. For loving what God allowed me to bring into this world. Beating me because I wanted to protect what was mine.

That night one of the older slaves comes to the shack and helps me with my open wounds. She helps me to stop the bleeding. The bleeding that you can see. The bleeding of my heart never stops. She told me to "Never let Master see you loving nothing, because that's the quickest way to get sold off." I don't care about being sold off, I don't care about nothing! The only thing I cared about was my little boy, and the white man has just stolen him from me.

For the next couple of weeks when I come in from the field I just lie on the dirt floor where me and Kwame laid and I just cry myself to sleep. I don't eat, and barely sleep; I just lie here thinking about my baby boy. I lie here and pray to God that he is okay.

Every time I get pregnant I think of the day Master sold my first baby away from me. How he beat me so bad for trying to hold onto my baby. How sick I was, that I couldn't eat, or sleep for weeks. I know they tell you to not be close to your babies because they will be sold off, but how can you carry a baby inside of you for months and not be close. Each and every time I had a baby it got taken away, and each and every time it broke me down.

I pray every night that somebody is loving on them and teaching them how to protect each other. I never knew so much pain. I really don't feel much of anything no more. Just empty. It's been a long time since I felt anything. I closed my head and my heart down many years ago. No sense in letting either one of them drive me crazy. I can't depend on my head or my heart anymore.

My new Master gives me to a new man now. They all call him Buck. Master makes us sleep together every night. I know he's waiting on Buck and me to make a baby. They say Buck has about 50 children! He said he never seen one of them never got a chance to hold or hug, or kiss not one of them. Now that right there is pretty sad! I did get a chance to hold my babies and love on 'em for a short while. But to never hold your child is downright pitiful.

Well night time comes and so does Buck. He comes straight to my shack. We sleep together like Master wants, but no baby! I think that maybe God is taking pity on me and Buck by not letting us have another child that will just be sold away from us.

Master can't believe I'm not pregnant yet. That really makes him mad at me and Buck. Some nights Master comes in to watch. He said he's making sure we doing it. I think he just like looking at us do it. By now I'm well past embarrassed, so it don't even bother me that Master is right here looking.

On the nights he don't send Buck in to my shack, he comes. He does his business to me and leaves. I just lay there. Too tired to cry, too broken to care, too scared to fight. Too done to give a damn!

After a year of Buck and Master both doing their business to me, Master tells me he's gonna sell me down the road because I'm too old and useless now.

I think I'm just about thirty something years old. Maybe thirty four, or thirty five. It's hard to remember. The days, months and years roll on with nothing to remember but agony and pain, and I try my best to forget all of it.

New plantation, new Master, same beatings, same despair.
I work in the house now, taking care of the little white children. I do all the cooking and cleaning and all the raising of the Master's children. Some days I hold that little baby child like she's my own; I was always afraid to let the Master see me loving on my own young ones. Quick as they see you love some body, they sell them off. So I just had to love my own in my heart and not show it.

So me holding the Master, and Misses baby real close makes me feel warm inside. I can't understand for the life of me how God can let white people have families and allows blacks to be separated everyday! Life sure ain't fair, not fair at all for black folks. Well I ain't gonna waste my time or brain trying to figure out God. God is gonna be God whether I understand or not. I just have to believe and trust in him, and I do.

The babies I care for are getting older now and Master says he gonna sell me to Master Pete down in Georgia. Master Pete is one honery white man! He's the kind of Master that nobody wants. Master Pete is poorer than most whites, but he still got slaves. Most of his slaves don't eat but once a day. He say he ain't gonna spoil no niggers by fattening them up.

They works from "can't see to can't see" on his plantation. Guess I don't have much say so bout being sold off though. The Misses likes how I've taken care of her little ones but said they getting too attached to me. I think the Misses is jealous that her own babies love me more than they love her. Don't know if they even like her much. She never spends time with them. She spends all her time with other white women having tea and laughing and talking and such.

I overheard her tell Master that I had worn out my welcome on this plantation. To be honest with you, I never even felt welcome here, not one day. Haven't felt welcome nowhere in America. Not welcomed, or wanted. I haven't felt welcome since I left my home in Africa.

So each and every day I wake up ready to go. I'm always ready to go. That's the life of a slave, stay ready to leave at any time, and don't get too attached to nobody! I learned these lessons early on.

Well, days and months pass and Master still ain't sold me off yet. So I just continue to run the house the best I can. I try to pull myself back from the children, so things will be better for them and me.

I guess it's a good thing that Master didn't sell me off because the Misses done took sick. She is really sick! So, now I'm taking care of her and her children. I sleep in the big house now seeing that the Misses is so sick I have to be close if she needs me.

One night she's freezing and cold and the next night she burning with the fever. I hold her hand and wipe her face and clean her when she messes herself. The old doctor said she ain't got long before she be dead and gone. Dr. said it's the fever she got. They called it the scarlet fever.

Now, the Master don't be here much no more. Just the Misses, me, and the children. Master Workman comes in early in the morning to eat and leaves as quick as he comes. Not once does he stop to look in on Missy Anne. He don't even look in on the children. I heard he was spending most of his time going from cabin to cabin to do his business with the young slaves he just bought. A few of the slaves, they say, are even Master Workman's own kids. They mama is a slave so they is a slave too. High yellow, but not white. Still a slave!

Well Missy Anne is lying awfully still tonight. She sweatin worse than ever before. I take a rag and dip it in the cool water and place it on her head to cool her down, I think that comforts her for a while.

I see fear in Missy Anne's eyes. I know fear. That's the same look of fear I saw from the people on the slave ship. I try to push those memories out of my mind, but they come back whenever they want to.

I sit here and hold Missy Anne's hand till she takes her last breath. She free now! I kinda wish it was me. Free!

I really don't know which cabin Master is in so I just go to the porch and ring the bell! The big porch bell is meant only for Master. He rings it when we can come from the field. I can't worry about that now though.

I ring it until he comes running! The whole plantation is woke. It's still dark of night but everybody is woke now.
Master runs right past me nearly knocking me to the ground. He rushes up to the bedroom where Missy Anne is but it's too late. She's gone! I rush in behind him to comfort the children.

Master tells me to wash Missy Anne up and put her in her best dress. He tells me to prepare her for her funeral. I never washed a dead person before but I did just as Master told me. I changed the bed covers too. She had soiled them. Once I washed her and cleaned the room Master brought the children in to say their goodbyes.

I don't know why my heart was breaking for the people that didn't care nothing for me, but it was. I felt tears rolling down my face as the children laid on their dead mama. They cried and kissed her until morning. I found myself crying right with them. My tears wasn't for the Misses though, my tears was for these babies I had helped to raise.

Next day Master Workman and some more white men bury Missy Anne down towards the river creek.

Master said nobody had to work the fields today in honor of Miss Anne. That made everybody happy! Everybody except me. I still had a lot of work to do. I cooked all morning until well past afternoon. Seeing that the Master had a lot of kin folk and friends visiting; the house was full all day long. People coming and going. Some happy, some sad. Some I believe just come by to be nosey. Checking all through Master's house.

Master did send for another young slave girl to come help me with the cooking and cleaning though. Her name was Felicia, and she looked just like Master Workman, but she was yellow, not white. So she still a slave.

Felicia was tall and thin. She was almost as tall as Master. She had real long reddish hair. It wasn't many slaves like her working the fields. They mainly work in the big house. They call them house slaves, and the rest field slaves.

I figured Master knew Felicia was his own daughter and he wanted to make her life as a slave a little bit easier. I don't think she could come inside the house while the Misses was still alive. That there is another whole long story about the Misses and Master Workman. That woman hated the sight of young slave girls.

I really didn't take to Felicia at first. Maybe I should say Felicia didn't take to me. I tried many times to talk to her, and even train her on the house ways, but she never listened to me. She just went on about the house like she was the new Misses. I think it was because she knew Master was her father. Even though he would die and be buried in his grave before he would claim her, or any of the other ones he had fathered.

A lot of masters had children by their slaves. They called it increasing their investment, or improving the livestock. And I'm here to tell you that Master Workman really increased his investment. They said he had twenty or so mulattos. That's what they called them. That was part African and part white. All sorts of colors, but all considered black. Not many of the people I see are as black as me, or any of my kinfolk back home. This plantation has lots of mulattos, a lot of black mixed with white.

A whole year done passed before Master brings home a new Misses.

Me, myself, I was happy because I thought she could be of some help with the Master and Missy Anne's little ones, but she surely wasn't! She never lifted a hand to help, and I don't believe she even carried on a conversation with them kids. Now that's just downright pitiful. Knowing that they mama was dead and gone, and she the new mama, you would have thought she would come in there and love all on 'em. Not this new Misses, nope she was not having any of that!

Now, poor Felicia wasn't nowhere near happy about the new Misses. She had been the lady of the house since Missy

Anne died. Many nights Master and Felicia would be doing their business as soon as I got the littles put down for the night. I always wondered how Master felt knowing he was doing his business with his own flesh and blood. He had to know that was his child even if she wasn't white as he was. Felicia had to know he was her daddy too. She was his spitting image. She looked more like him than his own claimed children, just had some black in her. It was no doubt about it, that Felicia was his own blood, and everybody knew that! I never knew how Felicia felt about it either, because she never stopped to say two words to me. She probably thought it was beneath her to be talking to a slave. She had it in her head that she wasn't one.

Now this new Misses, she is mean and nastier than the first one. I thought Miss Anne was vile but this one here even dirtier than her! She sends me and Felicia back to the fields.

I think going back out to the fields broke poor Felicia down worse than watching her mama get sold off! That poor mulatto child really believed she was gonna be the woman of this here plantation. I don't rightly know what Master was telling her while they were doing the business, but there was no way a black woman, even if she was high yellow, or mulatto was gonna be the woman of NO plantation!

Every night when the big porch bell ring to come back in for the night I goes over and help Felicia.

My heart kinda goes out to Felicia even though I know she

really never cared for me. Almost thought she hated the sight of me when we both worked in the big house.

She is quite a bit younger than me, but I'm much stronger. One day she actually turns and smiles at me for helping her. Some slaves just ain't cut out for slave labor. This field work, from "can't see to can't see," is awfully hard. It's hard work for a strong man and double hard for a woman. Us women folk have to do as much as the men folk out here in these fields. The young and small ones too. That day Felicia smiled was the first time that ever happened. The whole time we was in the big house she never even looked at me twice. It was many days back then that I helped her, but she probably felt it was just my job to do it. Out here my job and her job is the same as everybody else in this field.

The other day I saw that young girl Molly out here in the field working as hard as everybody else. Picking and packing cotton, and toting her bale. I just delivered her second child last week and she back out here working just as hard as she did before the baby come. We all know Master don't let you rest long at all. Once you have your baby you gotta get right back to the fields. A few of the older slaves tend the babies until the babies are old enough to walk along side their mama, and keep up with her. That's usually around about the age of 6 or 7 years old. Sometimes even as early as 5 years old!

A SHIFT CHANGE!

One night a couple of women folk run up to me and say Felicia done took real sick! So once I get to the shack where she's laying, it's a crowd of folk staring down at her. I make my way through the crowd and kneel down next to her to see what's wrong. Felicia is pale as a ghost. She shivering and sweating at the same time, just like Missy Anne did before she died. I get a shirt and tears it up, and start wiping the sweat from her face. Felicia turns and looks up at me and tries to smile. Now that's the second time she has smiled at me. I hold her close and begin to rock her like she's my own. All my babies were sold off from me, or I was sold off from them. So, I ain't rocked, or held nobody black in a long time. I been holding white babies since I got here though.

I guess with all the noise, it stirred Master because when I looked up he's walking in the shack now. He pushes past everybody to see what's going on. He wants to see what's all the commotion about. I tell him I believe Felicia done got that scarlet fever same as what Missy Anne had. I ask if I can take her up to the big house till she can get back on her feet again. Well, you would've thought I had asked Master for his first born child! He turned blood red and screamed and cursed me just for asking. I guess I should have known better, but I was just thinking of Felicia. I wasn't thinking that a black life don't matter on the plantation. Not a sick black person.

I Still Hear the Drums

Master did say that Felicia could stay in for a few days, but that was it! I guess that's more than some Masters would do. I've seen sick slaves fall dead in the fields before. That just made more work for the rest of us. They have to stop long enough to pick the slave up and bury him and get back to work.

That night when I leave the field I go by to check on Felicia. I make sure she eats and sometimes I hold her and rock her. She seems to really like that. She's a grown woman but grown or not, it's good to know somebody cares about you. She ain't got no mother around these parts, so I know she's glad to have me right now. I really like this time with Felicia seeing that I don't know where none of my own children are. Me and Felicia both look forward to this time in the evening. One night while I was caring for Felicia I began to tell her the story of my people. My people back in Africa. I told her about the elders that I still miss, the elders that I still love and respect, and all my kinfolk in our village.

I told her about the drums that you can hear being played all day and into the night. The drums that I still hear when I lie very still. The drums that I heard when they captured me and forced me onto the slave ship. I told her at night I lie very still and with my eyes closed and my heart open I can still hear the drums!

That night seems to have changed things between me and Felicia. Not only did she start to get better but our relationship did too. Felicia was up and back in the field after a couple of days. We always stayed close in the field and always walked back to our shacks together. We would eat together too.

It was kinda like having a real daughter I guess. I guess it was real comforting to her too. Most nights Felicia would ask me to tell her stories of my people and my home. I guess because this plantation was the only home she knew. Her mama never got a chance to tell her anything, so she took on my stories as her own. Sad to think that this plantation was all she knew.

One night she told me she had laid real still in her shack on the sackcloth dirt floor and prayed to hear the drum beats that I always talk about. She swore she actually heard, and felt them deep in her soul. I didn't question her either, because I still hear them and feel them deep in my soul too.

Many years have passed and I'm still here at the Workman plantation. I don't do much field work now. I just watch all the little children til they about six or seven years old. That's when they old enough to start picking and packing in the field with they mamas.

Felicia done had three children by now. All three of them children bring me some joy. Joy I never thought I would have on this side of life. Not after leaving my home and my people. Well these three children is like my family. It's like I'm they grandma! When I think about all this love I have and give them I always wonder how my own children are. I wonder did any of them have babies. I wouldn't know them if I was to pass them on the road. Real sad thought. But I do know these right here, and I love them with all I have, and they love me right back!

Two of Felicia's babies are smooth caramel color, the color of leaves before the snow season. One of the babies is almost as white as Master Workman. You can see him all over that boy's face. So he's that baby's daddy and granddaddy!! That's not my sin and not my problem. I love them all the same. I teach them all the things the elders taught me, like how to be strong, and how to be respectful and honest. I love these babies. I tell them all the stories of Africa. The stories of my home. The stories of my people. The stories of all of our people! Africa belongs to them too, they just don't know it yet.

I even tell them about that sad day I was captured. I tell them that I was a happy girl in my village; that all people don't live like this; that our people back home in Africa are free. I try to tell them exactly what free is, but they too young to really understand completely. But they sure do love to hear my stories! I have them lie still so we can listen for the drum beats from home. I tell them that Africa is a large continent, but every country there loves the drums.

Strangest thing is when I lie real still I sometimes can still hear, and feel those drums from home. I can still feel them in my soul!

My grandbabies say they can hear them too. I just look at them and smile. I think they just saying that to make their old granny happy. I just lie on this dirt floor next to my grandbabies listening to the drumbeats of home and I'm happy. Imagine that, me Abena Imari, or Beulah, found a little happiness. Hard to imagine happiness in this God forsaken place, but here I am smiling, and loving this time right here.

CHAPTER THREE

FREEDOM, NOW WHAT

Lately we been hearing a lot of rumbling and speculating. Some people happy, some people sad. Mostly we all just confused and scared. Scared because we really don't know what's going on! Every night when we leave the fields we all head to one cabin. It's where we can all be together. We sit and wait til mostly everybody is in then we begin to speculating again. Speculating on what Big Joshua told us.

Big Joshua always leads the conversation. Big Joshua is the Master's driver and he knows a lot about the things outside of the plantation. Things none of us ever dreamed of knowing. Big Joshua hears about slave comings and goings before the slave even know he's gotta go. So when Big Joshua talks, we all like to be close and listen.

Well, he promised us some news we wasn't gonna believe. He told us as soon as our work was done to meet up at the cabin. Well, we all are here waiting to hear the unbelievable news. The news he gives us nobody believes! You know what Big Joshua tells us? He tels us there's a war about to start between all the white folks. That the white folks is fighting each other! They calling it a Civil War.

There's the white man that want to stop slavery. Can you believe that!? Then there's the white man that don't want to stop slavery, they don't want it to ever end. I didn't know that any white man wanted slavery to end. They all seem mighty happy having slaves. They all seem extra happy beating and selling us off. Not to mention the real mean ones that like doing their business with us whenever they want to. What white man don't want slavery!

So when Big Joshua tells us this, not many of us slaves believe him. He knows it sounds crazy so he's grinning all the while he's telling it. Big mouth wide open with those four good teeth showing. He's just grinning and pacing back and forth as he tries to explain this here thang called the Civil War to us.

The white man up North fighting the white man down here in the South. The white men up North wants us to be free, but the white man down South on the plantations wants us to stay slaves.

Yeah this is pretty hard to believe. I'm scared to believe one white man will kill another white man to make us free. I'm scared to even think it because my heart been broke too many times to think something this wonderful could actually happen.

Big Joshua tell us all to keep right on working like we don't know nothing. That really ain't too hard for us to do, because none of us believe a word of it anyway! If we do believe it we too scared to show it.

Everybody goes back to their own shack after the big news. None of us say a word as we all walk back, everybody walking back in silence. Cat done stole all of our tongues, I guess.

When I get to my shack I lie there for what seems like forever, just lying there, mind racing, heart pacing! Just lying there thinking about freedom! I can't control my mind, it's running faster than ever now. Thoughts jumping in and out of my head like them little leap frogs, just jumping!

My thoughts keep going back to my family back in Africa, and my family spread to all parts of these United States. How can I go back home without my own children? I don't know where none of my babies are! They were all sold off many years ago. I got so many questions about freedom, and family, if this is true I pray my babies are about to be free too! Maybe the good Lord will direct me to my babies, that's if this rumor of freedom is even real.

I lie here thinking till the sun begins to come up. This is a real confusing time right now. I thought being a slave was confusing, but just thinking that we might be free, now that confuses me even more!

I done prayed for freedom ever since I was thrown in the bottom of that old slave ship. Now that was more than sixty years ago. More years a slave than most. Slave life is so hard not many people make it this long. Believe me, it ain't been easy. The good Lord must be keeping me around for some reason.

All that praying and now Big Joshua standing there with that big smile and one good eye, talking straight to my heart.

Joshua can see the future better than me. One eye or not that man never let nothing stop him.

Big Joshua comes to the Workman plantation shortly after I arrive. He comes on the back of a wagon, looking just about half dead. All bloody and dirty. His last master put his eye out when he talked back to him. Told him niggers gotta learn their place in these here United States.

Right after that he sold him to Master Workman. He was up and working after a day or two. Dried blood still on his head, face and clothes!

Master told Big Joshua he would put his other eye out if he ever talked back to him. I think most of the white men were scared of Big Joshua because he was really big and really strong. I think that's why they hated him so much. They hated to see all that power in one man. He didn't need no whip, or gun to be powerful. The white men were jealous of Big Joshua, and that's why they hated him so much.

Big Joshua was big but he was really gentle though. He could calm every horse from here to the next plantation.

He just had that way about himself. And he had a particular way with animals. I guess that's why Master made him his driver. We all thought it was kinda strange to have a one-eyed driver but nobody knew those horses like Big Joshua, and them horses listened to him too.

The next morning we all get to the field feeling a little excited and a whole lot of scared. The, "what ifs" keep coming up. What if it's true, and there is something called a Civil War? What if the side fighting for us to be free don't win? What will the white men down south do then? What if the good side, that's the side that wants us free, win and make us free? Then what? What does free look like in America?

So many "what ifs" makes my head start to spin again. Free, free, free, that's all I can think about all day today.

I speck that's what we all thinking about. Nobody says a word, but you can surely see it on they face now. Some looking mighty happy. Some looking mighty scared. I guess I'm looking a little of both, happy and scared. Looking a might tired too, seeing that I didn't sleep a wink last night. I can't wait to get back to my shack so I can think some more on this new thing called freedom. Lord, I pray you have it for us. Lord knows we been suffering a mighty long time now. I keep trying to quiet my heart. It feels like it's beating loud enough for everybody to hear it. I guess that's just what excitement will do to you. Been a long time since I had something to be excited about.

I know Big Joshua told us to act the same, but I can't get my heart to calm down!

Well, every night for the past week been pretty much the same. We all meet up in one shack and talk about freedom. Most all the slaves listen to me because I still remember freedom. Never had freedom over here though, but none of them have had freedom anywhere! All of them was born slaves and never got a chance to even know freedom. I pity this whole room of people that never know how it feels to wake up to birds singing, just a big bell on the Master's porch, is what they always had to wake up to. Sad they never got a chance to see their elders. Never got a chance to really belong to anything, or anybody. Real sad.

Well, if this Civil War they speculating about is so, and if the good whites win, then maybe they can get home and meet their elders. Now wouldn't that be something. Lord, Lord, Lord! All of us going back home. Them going for the first time, and me returning. Well there my heart goes, beating so fast I can't keep up with it.

CHAPTER 4

THE NEWS IS TRUE!

It's afternoon time and I don't know why Master Workman is ringing the bell this time of day for. Well, most people don't mind him ringing it, they just glad to come out of the field and rest for a while, and listen to him talk.

Once everybody is rounded up Master begins speaking. This time when he speaks his voice is shaky and trembling like I never heard before. Can't quite understand a word he's talking about, that is until he say the words Civil War! Did Master just say Civil War? Same as Big Joshua told us a week ago?

I look around at everybody standing in that field, waiting to see how they act, and we all act the same. We act like we ain't never heard of a Civil War. Master Workman begins to explain things to us, but it's nothing like what Big Joshua told us. Master say those men up North are mean scoundrels. I say to myself if they are meaner than these scoundrels down here I can't take it. Master tells all of the young strong boys and men to stay close he wants to talk to them some more. Then he sends everybody else back to work the fields.

Everybody walks back slowly, kinda in a daze. Big Joshua was right! There is a Civil War happening. There are people fighting to give us our freedom. Imagine that! Some white men actually fighting for us. Never thought I would live to see the day a white man would try to help a slave. I done seen it all now.

Well, I go back to watching the little ones as they mama's head back to work the fields. That sun is awfully hot beating down on everybody, but I speck nobody caring about how hot it is today. No sir, nobody worried about the heat! And me, I can barely wait until night time so we can all figure this Civil War thing out together.

Nobody comes to the shack tonight so I just sit up all night with my own thoughts; thoughts of Africa; thoughts of all my babies, wherever they are, and thoughts of the elders. My children will love the elders, just as I do. The elders can teach them the things I didn't get a chance to teach them.

The wake up bell rings and we all find our way outside. Master Workman is outside standing on the porch with three men behind him. One is my grandbaby Colby, the other two is white men I never seen before.

Colby standing there looking more like Master than Master do hisself! Standing there tall, lanky, and almost white as any other white man. He could pass for a white man any day. But he's black and all of us know it. He's black because his mama is black. Felicia is Colby's mama so he's still a slave.

Master comes down off the porch and commence to tell us that, the Civil War is getting close and he may be leaving for a little while and he is leaving these men behind him in charge until he gets back. I can't believe he's leaving Colby in charge. Colby is a slave like the rest of us. Many days Master brings Colby in the house and talks to him about a lot of things. I can overhear them when I'm in there cleaning up. I think that's why Colby don't realize he's a slave like the rest of us.

Master told us if anybody gets out of line they gonna be dead on the spot! Master said he's giving them permission to shoot us on sight with no questions! He said he's not gonna tolerate no slaves of his getting riled up over this crazy Civil War. He used some really bad words when he was talking. His whole face was blood red. Look like master had aged over night! This Civil War is killing Master, and he ain't even begun to fight.

After his speech we all head back to work. I turn back to look at Master as he hands my "grandson" Colby a gun!! And he handed him a whip too! Never thought I would ever see that happen. A white man hand a gun and a whip to a black man. All kind of things happening that don't even happen in dreams!

Well Colby takes the whip and the gun, and smiles, and follows the slaves to the field. I guess Colby is the new overseer. My, my, my, don't that break my heart.

That night when we all meet up for our Civil War and freedom talk, Colby don't come. Some people said Colby is worse than the Master, and the white overseers with that whip! Slapping on his own people! It breaks my heart to think this baby I helped bring into the world, and helped Felicia raise, is now beating his own people. Lord have mercy on him. That almost white skin color of his, done made him hate his own people.

Master stayed gone for only a few months before he come back to the plantation. It's sad to say some of the slaves would rather have Master than our own Colby. Well, we can't call him one of us no more. Colby really took to overseeing, so we don't think of him as one of us. He took to swinging the whip really fast. I think Colby forgot he was actually black. He stopped coming around any of us. Probably best he didn't come around because nobody trust him now. That really broke my poor Felicia's heart. Felicia tried talking to him about being so mean, when she heard how bad he beat his own brother! Colby and his brother Latham were different as day and night. Latham's daddy was a buck named Tommy. Master sold him off as soon as Felicia got pregnant. He beat poor Tommy something bad before selling him off. Master wanted to control who you did your business with. I guess he didn't know Tommy and Felicia had feelings for each other until Felicia got pregnant.

Standing there looking at Latham you could see Tommy all

over again. He was quite a bit lighter than his father Tommy. Latham was the color of a mixture of Felicia's high yellow and Tommy's stone black. That made him a smooth golden like color, the color of a warm sunset. Latham stood flat foot and strong. Much stronger than his older brother Colby. Seems funny how they played together every day as kids now Colby holds the whip in his hands and beats his own brother! Something I will never understand. Felicia went to the overseer's shack to ask Colby if he would be easy on his brother Latham, and Colby threatened to beat her if she questioned him about his handling of the slaves!! Colby pushed her out of his shack and told her to never return. I'm surprised he didn't beat her. Colby really had forgotten who he was, once Master Workman gave him a little power over the rest of us.

CHAPTER 5

THE CIVIL WAR

Well Master Workman comes back home to a big welcome home celebration seeing that he went and got injured in this Civil War. He comes home with just one leg! Ain't that a sight. Master hopping around on one leg. Having one leg made him twice as mean though. He said the slaves were making white men kill other white men, and that just wasn't right in his book. Don't know what book Master been looking in, but a lot of stuff I done seen and heard ain't been close to being right in my book.

Months pass without any change. Colby and the other two white overseers still running things while Master sits on the big porch drinking day in and day out.

One night as we all sitting around talking, Big Joshua say the Civil War needs black folk to help fight for our own freedom. How we gonna do that. We all saying it at the same time. The white men got all the guns. Well, Big Joshua say the white men up North gonna let the slaves fight! Gonna give them guns and pay them too! Now this is too much for any of us to even try to believe; but Big Joshua ain't never told us wrong before.

He told all the young strong men that the Union soldiers gonna need them real soon! The Union soldiers is the ones from up North trying to free us, and the Confederates is the ones down South fighting to keep us slaves. With all this talk about Union and Confederates, up North, and down South, my head starts to spinning!

We got more questions than Big Joshua got answers for.

Latham was the first one to speak up and say he's gonna fight. Said he wants a gun and as soon as he can, he's going off to fight for all of us, in this Civil War!

After some time passes Master starts to selling off a lot of the older slaves. I keep thinking every morning he gonna call me up to the porch and tell me I done been sold. It keeps a knot in my stomach not knowing. I've been on this plantation longer than I been any other place in my whole entire life. Been here longer than I was even at home. Home in Africa.

This place is the closest thing to home, and these people are the closest thing to family that I've known, in a very long time. Now everyday a wagon pulls up and take some of my plantation family off to who knows where. It hurts my heart but I'm use to Master selling off people. They always selling off people you grow too close to. You can't allow yourself to love nobody around here. Soon as you do, Master snatch 'em away and sells 'em off real quick!

Every time I see Latham he's talking about this Civil War. He can't stop thinking about it, or talking about it. Well one night Latham comes to my shack to say goodbye, it took everything I had not to break! When he said goodbye, part of my heart leaped with joy and the other part withered with fear.

Latham said the Union soldiers are close. He heard they were over at the next plantation and he's ready to join up with them. I kissed Latham and told him be safe, and I was pretty proud of him.

Latham and five or six more men, and boys left that night to meet up with the Union soldiers. It was hard to keep my mind off of Latham and the men and boys that left. I worried myself sick over them. They left to fight for our freedom and I was mighty proud, but I was mighty scared too.

I wondered if any of my own children, or grandchildren were somewhere fighting for our freedom. That would make me so proud, I know my elders would be proud too!

Problems on the plantation.

Well when the word got out that Latham and the others had left to join up with the Union soldiers, Master tried to kill all of the rest of us that was left behind! He had Colby and a few white men to beat all the men from sun up to sun down. They even beat some of the women folk. He didn't even care about the fields that day. That was the bloodiest day I've ever seen. The next day I had to tend to all them wounds. The whole time I'm praying that Latham done met up with the Union men. Master say he's sending men and dogs to catch all the runaways. He promises to kill them dead on the spot. I do believe Master would rather sell them than kill them though.

Months pass we don't hear nothing from Latham so I believe he did meet up with the Union soldiers and is out there somewhere fighting to make all of us free. Latham is now in that Civil War!

Some days my heart say he's fighting, then other days my heart say them slave catchers done caught him and killed him on sight. Every night I pray for Latham and all the rest of us here suffering. I pray that my family that's scattered around this part of the world is doing the best they can. I still pray for my family back home in Africa. I wonder if they still think of me. I know most of the elders have gone on to the everlasting place. The ones still living, I wonder do they ever think about me. Ever wonder what ever became of me. Do I ever cross any of their mind. Not one day has passed since I was forced on that slave ship that I don't ask GOD to take care of them. I think of my home and my people every day. I used to think about home so much until I would almost get that same sick feeling I got when I was in the bottom of that old slave ship.

CHAPTER 6

THE BIG NEWS

EMANCIPATION PROCLAMATION

Well the few of us that are still left here on Master Workman's plantation is sitting around talking and listening to the wind blow late at night when the plantation bell starts to ringing. We all know that means get up to the plantation porch with no tarrying. So we gets there fast as we all can. We all rushing to see why Master ringing the bell this late at night.

My, my, my, what Master say to us that night like to surely take my entire breath away!

Master say some words I don't understand and we don't have Big Joshua around to explain it. Big Joshua was loaned out to do some driving for the white man on the next plantation. He won't be back for days, or maybe even months.

Well, we all standing there in the pitch black of night, all confused. Everybody confused as Master hold up a kerosene lamp and commence to reading a paper he said it's called the Emancipation Proclamation! All I know is once he was done reading it he say all y'all is FREE!

Free to go, free to be, free like the white man!

Master look worse than he did the night his mama died! This here Emancipation Proclamation damn near done killed Master Workman. I wonder if all the other masters is as sick as he is about this Emancipation Proclamation. Well all of us begin to cry, sing, laugh, and dance! The whole plantation looks different now. It don't look so scary. I look around for Felicia and don't see her nowhere. Everybody is heading over to the main shack so we can talk and learn what to do next. What does free even mean? Does that mean I can go back home now? After all these years I can go home? Abena Imari, NOT Beulah, is on her way back home to Africa! I'm scared to even think it could happen. Scared to get my hopes up like that.

When we get over there to the shack Felicia's already there looking scared and not at all happy like the rest of us. I goes over real close to her and I puts my arm around her to comfort her like I always do when she looks afraid. She seems like she cold and shivering something terrible. I just hold her a little tighter. Before anybody starts to talk Felicia's baby boy named Gabriel stands up and shouts out he's leaving as soon as the sun comes up. He said he heard we all should head up north where we can be safe. He said just because we free don't mean we safe. Gabriel said there's white men out there waiting to catch us and keep us in the secret slavery. LORD have mercy on us! Now what is the secret slavery I say? Gab said that's when the white man keeps you from freedom but say you can go if you want to go. They have the men with dogs waiting on you to bring you right back! We all look real confused now. I look over at Felicia and she looks white as a ghost. Felicia never had much color to begin with, but the little she had done drained right out of her face. She leans in and tells me she wants to stay here with Master on the plantation. She said Colby told her they would be fine to stay if they wanted to. Said Master had already told Colby all about this here Emancipation Proclamation. Felicia said Colby and Master done already worked out a deal where she can stay on and cook and clean at the big house, and Colby can be his driver. Guess they already had them some plans worked out. The rest of us still trying to figure all this out. Master knew Big Joshua wasn't gonna be coming back here once he heard about us being FREE.

Felicia is real sad because she knows Colby and her probably the only ones that might be safe. Colby and Felicia could pass for white any day. She sad because she knows in her heart her other kids may not fare as well. Her other kids will probably always have it hard even if they are free.

FREEDOM

What does freedom mean to a black person in America:

Most of us stay on the plantation and work as sharecroppers. That's where we all doing pretty much the same job we did before, except Master don't ring no bell and he supposed to pay us; we still waiting. We all living in the same shacks and eating the same slop. Every now and then Master gives us a little money, not enough to do anything with it, but it does feel good to have it in your hands!

Everyday new people comes up to the plantation looking for work. Asking if they can work the field for money or food. After the Emancipation Proclamation, a lot of people took whatever belongings that they had and struck out looking for a better life; a life where they were free to come and go as they chose. Some people stop by here long enough to get their strength up to head North. That's all you hear folks talk about is heading up North. Sound like North is the promise land for us Black folks. Down South, the white man still treating the blacks like slaves and we supposed to be free like they free; but we know our freedom ain't nothing like the white man's freedom.

I just fills my days trying to figure out how I'm gonna go about finding all of my children. I can't even begin to know where they are. One thing I know for sure is they nowhere around here. My babies was sold off on them other plantations I worked on. Sold off as little babies, sold off right from under me, like they wasn't even mine. Like I didn't carry them in my belly and birthed them into this world. Like they didn't even belong to me.

Even if by some miracle from GOD I did find all my babies how we gonna get all the way back home to Africa. I got seven grown children somewhere in this GOD forsaken country and only the good LORD knows where. I may have some grandbabies too by now. I'm pretty sure I do. Grandbabies I never got a chance to lay my eyes on. Closest thing I got to family is Felicia and her children. Felicia's children are my "grandbabies". I helped her birth the babies each one of them. I held them even before she did. I love them like they was my own. I even love Colby. I know deep in his heart he loves me too. Colby just confused that's all. Walking around with damn near white skin, but got a black soul. Kinda hard for him to know which side to be on. He gotta take the white side to stay safe. Yeah, I love Colby because living here in America the white skin is the safest skin to have. I know when Colby is alone to himself he thinks about being black and looking white. Gotta be a constant fight on the inside of him. So I love him, and I pity him too.

Been a lot of really long days and really long nights since I took sick. I stay in the cabin all day now. No sharecropping, no watching the little ones, just lying here on my cot, tired and sick most of the time. Tired, sick and old. Just lying here day in and day out lying here thinking about home. Thinking that one day I'm going home now that we all free. I ask everybody do they know how I can get myself back to Africa. Nobody around here ever laid eyes on Africa. All they know is America and slavery. I feel sorry for all of them. When I think about all the beautiful places at home that they never seen before. I guess I feel sorry for myself too. Sorry that I ain't there no more. I wish Big Joshua was still around, he always had answers. He probably could help me find my way back to Africa. Maybe even help me find all my family over here in America.

Well back to thinking and planning. I done saved up every dime Master give me for sharecropping. I hope it's enough to get back home to Africa. If a ship can get me just to the shore I can find my way home.

I will listen for the drums. Those drums will lead me back home. I still lie real still at night after everybody done quieted down, no screams or hollering, just the wind coming thru the cracks of this shack. I lie here and listen for the drums, the drums of home. Some nights I can hear them just as clear as if I was right there in my village! Some nights it's real faint, and most nights I can't hear them at all. I lie there every night though, with the same hope I had on that old slave ship. The hope that I will soon return home to my country, and return to my people. A lot of nights I make myself believe it will happen. Now, as I lie here on this cot on this dirt floor I truly believe I will return home to Africa. Just the thought of going back home now makes my heart beat fast and I find myself smiling. Smiling because I'm going home. Home after all these years. Home after all the beatings and tears. Then my smiles quickly fades when I think about my very own children, that I don't know where in this world they are. I hope and pray somebody loved on them like I did Felicia and her children. I hope they can make it up North where they say life is better and easier for us blacks.

I pray that the GOD of all things is always watching out for them. It's been so many years since I seen any of my babies, I'm sad to say that I wouldn't know any of them today. Each one of my babies got sold off as soon as they was big enough to go out to the fields. Most kids go to the fields around six or seven years old, some sooner if the Master think they can keep up. Breaks my heart seeing them babies out there in the high sun picking cotton. Them big cotton bags be bigger than them babies out there toting 'em. LORD what kind of people can beat down some poor little babies?

Time passes and I'm still here. Still on the Workman plantation. Now it's funny how life is, because now Felicia comes and takes care of me! She brings me food every day. She fusses at me when I don't eat. She just fussing because she loves me and I know it. She stays long as she can, and always come back at night. Felicia sometimes lies down right beside me. We both quiet, just lying here close, and quiet. I lean over and tell Felicia I really don't think I can make that long journey back home to Africa. When I tell Felicia that, she hugs me real tight and says, yes you will, you will return to Africa! I don't believe it, and I don't think Felicia believes it either, but she sure does sound convincing though. I believe the thought of me not returning to Africa brings Felicia as much pain as it does me. She has listened to me talk about Africa, and my elders, and hearing the drums for so many years now, that me giving up on my hopes of returning home hurts her heart.

I'm old now and real weak, I tell her that, but she don't want to hear it. So we just lie there quiet and still, just happy to be close to somebody that you love, and you know loves you. In the middle of our quiet time Felicia sits up and yells out that Latham is alive and sharecropping in the fields not too far from here! Said Latham is married now and got some babies of his own. Seems like I'm always happy and sad at the same time. This time I'm happy to know that my grandbaby Latham is alive. We hadn't heard anything from Latham since he left going to help fight in the Civil War. The war that freed us. Then sadness comes when I think that Latham is still down South. I hoped he would be up North living a better life than the rest of us in the mean old South. Some days down South you can't even tell that you really free. Can't tell that the Emancipation Proclamation meant anything to these white folks. I hear the white folks up North are a whole lot different than the ones down here.

Earlier than the sun comes up I hear somebody coming in the shack. I raise myself up to look at the face of the most handsome man I'd ever seen. Standing big and tall and brown, right before my eyes was Latham. The boy I held, rocked and fed. Felicia's boy was back! Standing right here before me! Standing here a man, strong and handsome. He rushes over to me to help me up off the cot. His arms are big and strong as he picks me up with no trouble.

Latham got that same big smile, he always had such a beautiful smile. You could just see the love in him when he smiled. Now he's smiling and I start to smiling too. We both happy as can be to be together again. Latham walks out of my shack and returns with three little ones that look just like him. Each one a different shade of brown, but looking just like their daddy. Each one just as pretty as the next.

Soon as Latham tells them I'm grandma they all rush straight over to me and hug me tighter than I been held in many years. Standing there looking at Latham and holding his babies I start to cry. This time not from sadness but sheer joy. Joy that Latham is okay, joy that his babies is beautiful, and loving, and they loving me. Yes this time these here tears are tears of joy. They call these happy tears.

Latham has to peel them babies off my legs. He tells me he will be back soon and bring the babies and his wife. I can't wait to meet Latham's wife, but mostly I can't wait to hold the babies close to me again.

CHAPTER 7

GOODBYE TO AFRICA

I wake up every day now knowing that I won't ever return home. I'm old and barely get from cot to door now. I know there's no way I can make it all the way back to my home. That beautiful place is just a distant memory now. The waves of sadness come all the time now. They come and stay. Sometimes I lie here sad just like I was many years ago on the old slave ship. I'm sad now because all those years I stayed strong knowing that I would return to Africa! Return home and tell all of my people how strong I was. Tell them they could be proud of me. Tell them I never forgot them. I never forgot the smell of the flowers, never forgot the sounds of the birds, the taste of our food. The touch of their hands, but most importantly I never forgot the sound of tribal drums. Those drums that are in my head and through my soul. The sound of those drums that kept me connected to them all these years. I wanted to tell them I still hear the drums. I heard them all the way across the waters and into a new world. A new world, but the same drum beat. I guess it's never going to happen now.

Early one morning just like Latham promised, I see him and his babies and a fine woman walking up the road directly toward my shack. I can't hide the joy that's welling up inside of me right now. Pure joy at seeing Latham and his babies. Once they all gets a little closer, they all begin to run. Running straight to me. I can see a big old grin come across Latham's face. I smile right back. Once Latham reaches my shack he grabs me and almost lifts me off the ground. Everybody laughs at the sights of me darn near in the air! We all hug and kiss and hug some more! Latham breaks the hugging up so he can introduce his wife to me. Latham clears his throat and says Grandma Beulah, this here is my wife Marie, we call her "Ree" for short. Then this real pretty woman smiles and stepped closer to hug me. I can see why Latham chose Marie. She about the prettiest woman I've seen since leaving my home. Her skin is smooth and dark. Dark light midnight, with no stars shinning. Her eyes are bright and she's got a smile to match. A real warm welcoming smile. Yeah, I see exactly why Latham chose Marie.

Now just as soon as we break from our hug, the babies begin grabbing and hugging on me again. I'm overjoyed today even with the thought of never going back home in the back of my mind. Right now I'm just gonna enjoy my family. Latham, "Ree" and his babies stay way up into the day, before Latham says it's time to go; says he's got a lot of work to do. I hug and kiss everyone of 'em before they take off, and Latham says he'll be back soon. I believe he will. He tells me he wants me to come with him when he comes back. Latham said he wants me to live with him and his family! Said I can help with the little ones while him and "Ree" do their sharecropping. Told me to think about it and let him know when he comes back. I told him I would think about it, but I knowed then and there I would most definitely go with Latham and his family. I helped Felicia raise him so he's the closest thing to family that I got. Latham IS family. Only the good LORD knows where my own children are. All of them grown and I suppose they got children and grandchildren of their own by now.

I'm all packed up just watching day turn into night and night turn back into day. Just sitting here waiting on Latham to come and fetch me. Whatever day he decides to come, I'll be ready, that's for sure.

When Felicia stops by to check up on me, I tell her I'm leaving, and we both hold each other and cry! A lot of years me and Felicia done spent together so we both a little sad. I remember the day when Felicia and me began to love each other. We started off kinda shaky at first, but the love shined right on through after a while. The good LORD knows I love Felicia and all of her family. They my family. Not true blood family, but family all the same.

CHAPTER EIGHT

A BRAND NEW HOME

Today's the day! I don't have much to move but Latham and a few others around here load it all up on a wagon. I stand up long enough to hug everybody and kiss all the little ones. My sweet Felicia is the last one to come over to me. She holds me real tight with tears running down her face. Her face is red and full of tears before she even gets close to me. I tell her we gonna see each other again and she just nods her head, squeezes my hand real tight, then quickly walks off.

When they gets me up in the wagon, I'm smiling from ear to ear! Gonna leave this place for good! Gonna be spending the rest of my days with Latham and his family. My family!

We come up on a big nice cabin. This cabin is bigger than any I've ever seen before. "Ree" is standing on the front stump with one baby in her arms, while the others run straight out to meet us. "Ree" flashes that big warm smile and I smile all the way to my soul.

Once I'm settled in "Ree" and Latham leave to tend the field. Sharecropping is just like slavery, but we don't have no master telling us what to do and when to do it. If you don't tend no fields you don't eat. I'm real proud of "Ree" and Latham, they tends the fields and raise all these younguns up right.

When night time comes they all comes straight to me to hear me ramble on about my old life. My life before slavery. I've told these stories so much ain't no way I could forget a single one. "Ree" said she knew a man from her old plantation that was from Africa, but she didn't know much else about him. Said he was really old and sick, said he didn't talk much, and when he did talk nobody understood him. She believes he died not long after she got to that plantation. I told myself he probably died of a broken heart. If I didn't have all these people in my life right now I probably would die too. Sad that he's dead and gone, I would love to see somebody from home. Anybody. Just one person, even if they were from another village. Just see somebody that could know exactly how I feel being over here in America.

You know the sun comes up really fast when you ain't sleeping. Most nights I'm just lying here thinking of home. This is the happiest I've been since I was back in my village. Lying here and my heart seems to beat faster. Seems like it's beating to the sounds of my tribal drums. I hear them almost every night now. I just lie still listening.

Latham's little ones lie next to me the whole time. I share a cot with the two youngest ones, Beverly and Chloe. They both rush to bed every night just to hear my stories! Watching them get soo excited, makes me excited to tell them same stories over and over again. The whole family gathers around each night to hear the old African stories. I tell them the stories of the ship, the people on the ship, both African, and the whites. I tell them how we were all chained together in the bottom of that filthy slave ship. I almost get sick just thinking of the smell, and the sickness, and the death of that ship; the smell of vomit, and urine that could almost take your breath away.

Latham done heard these stories all his life and he listens just like everybody else. He listens like it's his first time hearing them. I done told my African stories so much that now all the children can tell the stories to me! Sometimes I overhear them telling my stories like it actually happened to them. It warms my heart to hear them saying the things I said to them. Warms my heart to know they really are listening to this old African lady. I do believe that little Chloe thinks she was once over in Africa with me! Her bright eyes get so big, and she starts talking extra fast when she tells the Africa stories. I close my eyes and just listen. Chloe talking like she actually seen the beauty of Africa! Listening to Chloe makes me a little sad, but really proud too. I'm sad because my home is only a far off memory now. I know in my heart, that I'm too old, weak, and feeble, I'll never make it back home. I might not make it back but I feel the stories of home will carry on. Chloe, just like her daddy Latham, has taken on the old stories and will pass them on to generations to come! Never forget Africa is what I tell them all the time. Never forget you all got family over there across these waters. We got family over there that is surely sad like me. Sad, because the white man took us from them. Sad, because they know they ain't ever gonna see us again.

I know all of my elders are all gone to the resting place with the ancestors now but I hope the stories of how all of us were taken from Africa are being told with the ones still there. I hope they didn't forget about us. I pray all their hearts didn't break too bad when we left. I pray for the ones that get to return. I used to dream of the day that I would return home. I dreamed it would be a big deal to everybody in the village. Even the people in other villages would be excited to see that I made it back home. I'm not sure how many people had come out to see me; everybody though, including all the Chiefs, and Kings are there celebrating. We would dance and sing all day into the night. Dancing to the drum beat, that I NEVER stopped hearing.

Those dreams and the frequent sounds of my tribal drums are what kept me many days, and many nights.

The drum beat that kept me alive all these years in this foreign country. This country they call America. The country where me and people that look like me are broken beyond repair, beaten with no remorse and killed every day. You are sometimes killed for no reason at all; just because you are black. A country where the ladies is forced to have babies so their Master can claim more slaves.

Yeah, I dream of going home so I don't have to live this life no more. Then every morning I wake up, I find myself still here. Still praying for some kind of miracle. A miracle from God. A miracle from the ancestors, something, anything that will help me get back home.

CHAPTER NINE

LAST DAYS

They don't have no doctors for black folk, so when we get to ailing we use whatever we got to help with our situation. Lately I've been sicker than ever before. I don't get out of bed at all now. Just lie here in the same spot. My strength done gone, never to return. Sometimes I hear things, and see things that nobody else do. I remember some of the elders was like this. When I was a young girl back home I would hear them talking to air, just like somebody was there talking back to them. I remember people saying that the ancestors were close by, and they were close to death. They said the ancestors were talking to them and leading them on to the great after life. The thought of the ancestors coming for me don't scare me one bit! I welcome all of them. I've been tired and sick for a long time now, so if they ready for me, I guess I'm ready for them.

Felicia comes by every now and then, and tries to get me to eat a little something. She keeps a cool rag for my head. Felicia holds me and rocks me just like I did her when she got sick with that scarlet fever. Funny, how life works like a full circle.

Today I hear a lot of voices, but don't see nobody. I can recognize some of what they are saying. I think I hear my own mama talking now! I don't tell nobody because they can't hear them, just me. I'm the only one who can hear the voices. I believe it's my elders, and old ancestors talking to me!

Today Latham don't go to the fields. The whole family stays home. This ain't never happened before. Even Felicia comes back today. They all stay real close to me. Chloe moves in even closer. She starts talking softly, then she starts patting ever so softly on my hand. She's patting to the beat of my drums.

Tears rolling down everybody's faces. Everybody but me seems sad. I'm happy! Happy because I know what's coming next. I know what's about to happen.

Heaven is waiting and I'm ready. I been down here a mighty long time. I don't rightfully know exactly how long but it's more than 80 years I know. Eighty or so years full of sadness, heartache, and death. I did have some joy in them years though. Joy in all them that are here with me now, and joy for a short time with my own babies, before they got sold off. I had some joy back home in Africa too.

Now Latham done crawled up on the cot next to me and starts to rocking me like a baby. I haven't felt this comfortable since leaving home. Latham is strong like my elders. They would be proud to know him, and even prouder to claim him for our village.

All the while that Latham is holding me in his arms, his tears are dropping slowly on my face. I want to tell him everything will be okay, but I don't have the strength, and don't have my voice anymore. I just look him straight in the eyes and hope he can see what my heart is saying. My heart is telling him to be strong. The elders and now the ancestors will take it from here. I love you Latham. I love all of you, I always did, and I always will.

CHAPTER TEN

THE DRUMS USHERING ME HOME

Little Chloe starts telling me one of my old African stories, as I drift in and out. She's telling the story to me, just like I've always told it. Then she sits straight up in the bed. She jumps to the floor and looks around the room at everybody. She has a strange look on her face.

Chloe whispers, "Do you hear that?" Shh, shh, do you hear that daddy? Mama, Grandma Felicia do any of you hear that? They all look at each other all confused. Then Chloe and Little Latham both are standing in the middle of the room stomping their feet to the sound of the drums. They both can hear the drums!

The last thing I remember before I closed my eyes for the last time was Chloe and Little Latham actually feeling the drums. As I drift away I hear the drum beat stronger and stronger.

I STILL HEAR THE DRUMS!

EPILOGUE

So through it all, good times, and bad, the drum beats from home sustained me. From that slave ship, to freedom, and on into the Great forever, I heard the drums.

The sound of my tribal drums that pumps through my heart, and soul, kept me!

These were the sounds that always connected me to home!

"I STILL HEAR THE DRUMS"

AFRICA IN PICTURES

The following pictures are some of my favorites from my many visits to the African continent. Enjoy!

- Linda Lewis-Everett

Live ♥ Laugh ♥ Love

A few of the Lewis Group- Chester and Daisy's Kids

Cape Coast Castle 2018

Dubois Everett, in front of the Door of no Return

Dubois Everett, in front of the Door of no Return

Cape Coast Castle on my 2018 visit to Ghana

Linda Lewis-Everett in South Africa 2010

Beautiful Sky in Accra, Ghana 2018

Village in Kumasi, Ghana 2018

Village in Ghana 2018

Linda, and Debra in front of the Presidential Palace in Africa 2010

Linda in Accra, Ghana
in front of the Black Star Stadium
2018

Linda Lewis-Everett
Ghana 2018

Linda and Dubois Everett at the W.E.B Dubois Museum
Ghana 2018

Dubois in front of the President Kwame Nkrumah Statue. 2018

Drumming while in Ghana!
2018

Linda Lewis-Everett
Elmina Castle Dungeon
Ghana 2018

Inside the Slave Dungeon, with Regina Majors
Ghana 2018

Emotional visit inside the Slave Dungeon in Ghana 2018

Dubois Everett, in front of the Door of no Return

Dubois Everett at the Slave Last Bath
Ghana 2018

EMOTIONAL VISIT
Linda Lewis-Everett honoring my ancestors by dipping my hands in the Slave Last Bath 2018

In Ghana creating my own Andinkra sash

Linda Lewis-Everett standing in front of the Great Pyramids in Egypt/Kemet 2018

Linda Lewis-Everett riding the camels around the Great Pyramids in Egypt/Kemet 2018

Family photo overlooking Cairo, Egypt
Constance Clark, Gloria Vaughn, Dubois and Linda
Everett 2018

Cape Coast Castle 2018

Marital Vow renewal Dubois and Linda Everett 2018 Sisimbo Beach Ghana

Linda Lewis-Everett in Cairo, Egypt 2018

Linda Lewis-Everett in front of the Nelson Mandela Home/Museum 2010

Cape Point South Africa 2010

In Senegal Africa
in front of the LIBERATION statue 2010

Debra overlooking the vast ocean 2010

Approaching Gore'e Island 2010

Table Mountain South Africa 2010

Capetown 2010

Debra, inside the Slave Dungeon 2010

Linda, and Debra in South Africa 2010

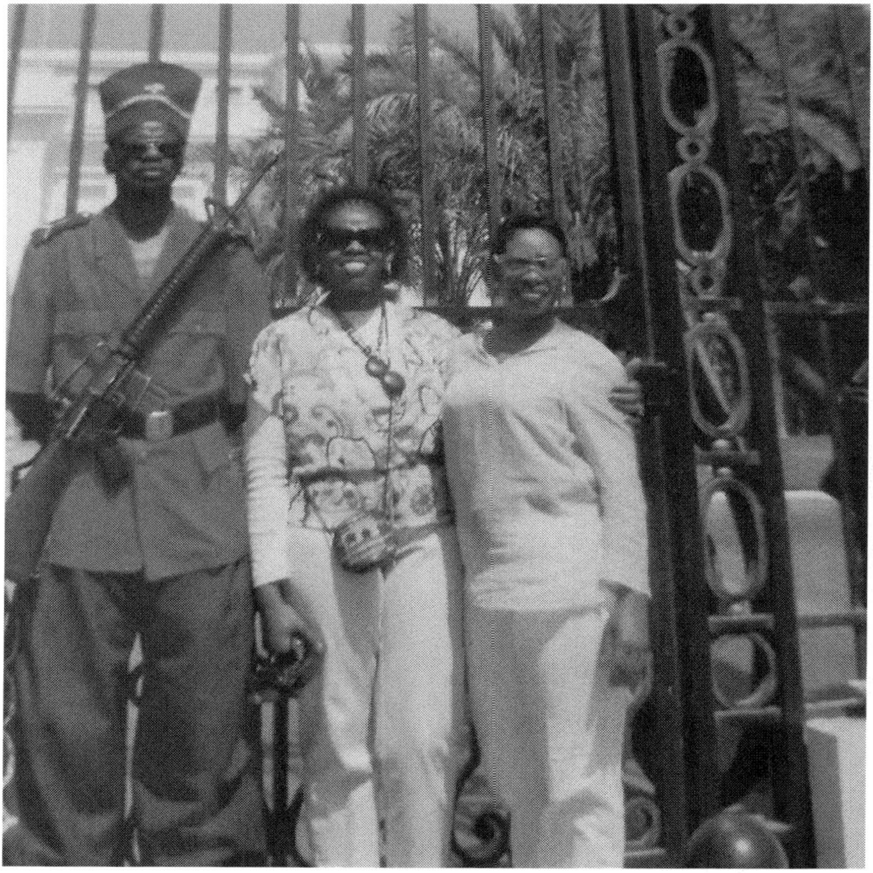

Mandela Family Museum
8115 Ngakane Str. Crn. Vilakazi
Orlando West Soweto
P.O. Box 7299 JHB. 2000
Tel. (011) 936 • 7754
Fax. (011) 936 • 4244
E Mail:

Small African Church in SOWETO 2018

Sitting on a "Whites Only" bench in the APARTHEID museum 2010

Delores, and Lana walking through the desert 2018

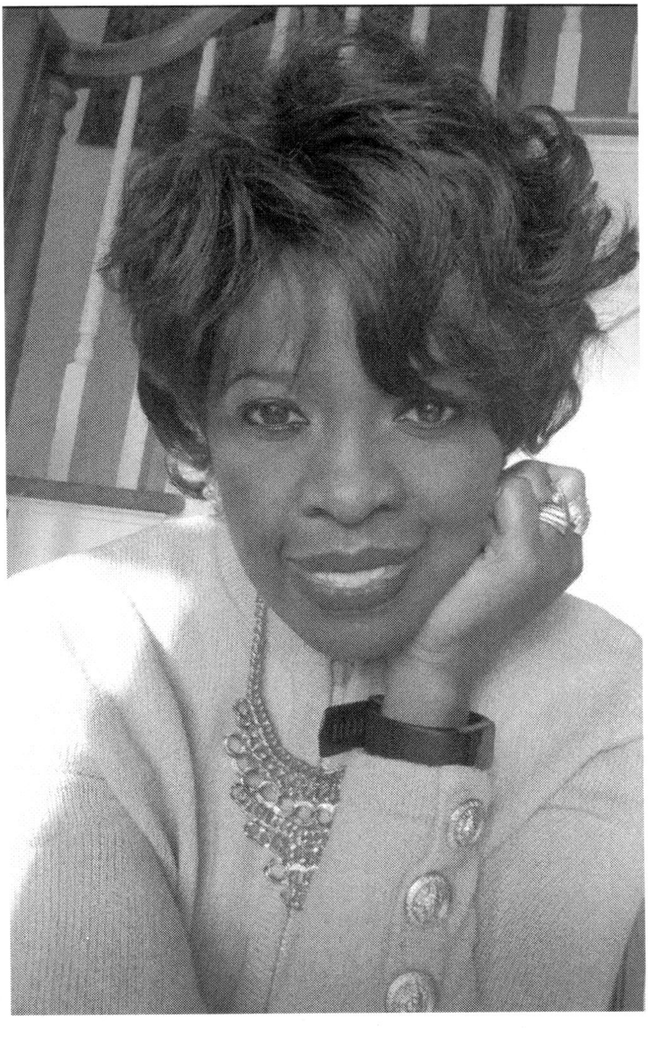

Linda Lewis-Everett

Linda Lewis-Everett is a native of Indianapolis and has been married to her husband, Dubois Everett over 28 years. They have one son, Kenneth Anthony Peters, and one granddaughter, Jala Nicole Peters.

Linda is a member of many civic, and social organizations, is engaged in many volunteer activities and she is an Advocate for the American Cancer Society. She is also a Proud Army Veteran. Linda enjoys traveling, shopping, gardening, and reading. Linda shares a strong kinship with her African roots, has visited Africa multiple times and that kinship provided the inspiration for this novel.